To Fred, George, and Thomas, my pirates in pajamas,

and Christopher—the captain of our ship.

~ C. C.

For Archie, Seth, and Tabby

~ T. K.

tiger tales
5 River Road, Suite 128, Wilton, CT 06897
Published in the United States 2015
Originally published in Great Britain 2015
by Little Tiger Press
Text copyright © 2015 Caroline Crowe
Illustrations copyright © 2015 Tom Knight
ISBN-13: 978-1-58925-190-8
ISBN-10: 1-58925-190-3
Printed in China
LTP/1400/1136/0315
10 9 8 7 6 5 4 3 2 1

For more insight and activities,
visit us at www.tigertalesbooks.com

PIRATES in PAJAMAS

by Caroline Crowe   Illustrated by Tom Knight

tiger tales

Do **pirates** wear pajamas
when it's time to say good-night?

Do they have a skull and crossbones?
Are they **striped** in **black** and **white?**

No! When pirates choose pajamas
they're not always what you'd think:

Some are **purple**,

some are **orange**,

some are **yellow, green,** or **pink!**

There are knitted ones
with **pom-poms,**

ones with **spots** and
frilly sleeves;

Some are **fluffy**
all-in-onesies,

and some hang
down to the **knees.**

If you board the *Leaky Parrot*
  just before you go to bed,
Captain Redbeard's on the poop deck
  with a snorkel on his head.

He jumps into the bathtub,
tossing **bubbles**
everywhere.

His crew are making shark fins
with the shampoo in their hair.

AYE
AYE
WAX
Finest eye patch
Polish

Fancy
Hair
Oil

BOOTY
BUBBLES

"Grab your towels!

the Captain cries, "and dry behind your knees.

POWDER

"The last one in pajamas
smells like **stinky, moldy
cheese!**"

Rotten Roger's pj set looks good enough to eat;

and **Hank** has
fancy feet!

Sneaky Pete's
have dancing cats,

Captain Redbeard's onesie
must have shrunk a size or two;

He can't close up the buttons,
and his tummy's **poking**
through!

Pirates throw pajama parties
almost every single night.
They parade their **jazzy jammies**
and have pirate . . .

Wallop, whack, white feathers fly,
and tickle everywhere.
Hank laughs so hard
his jammies slip . . .

. . . and leave

his **bottom**

bare!

Dressed for bed, they drink their milk
and start to close their eyes.

And tucked in tight,
they drift to sleep . . .

...to pirate lullabies.

Zzzzzz

Zzzzzz

Zzzzzz

So if you want to be a pirate,
you don't need a patch or sword.

You just need your
best pajamas,

and a bed to
climb aboard.